ALL★STARS

Written by Mark Vancil

A GOLDEN BOOK • NEW YORK

Western Publishing Company, Inc., Racine, Wisconsin 53404

The Slam Dunk

   Professional basketball has been around since the early 1900s. But basketball's most exciting play, the slam dunk, did not become an accepted move until the 1960s.

   Instead of shooting the ball from the outside or banking a shot off the backboard, players use one or both hands to slam the ball through the basket. Although many players could dunk in the 1950s, few ever did. They thought dunking was showing off.

   Then Wilt Chamberlain joined the Philadelphia Warriors in 1959. At 7-foot-1, Wilt "the Stilt" was the tallest player in the game. He could almost touch the basket without jumping. The dunk was one of his best moves.

   The dunk became so popular that the National Basketball Association, or NBA, started competitions in 1984. The Gatorade Slam-Dunk Championship takes place every year during the All-Star Weekend festivities.

Wilt Chamberlain, 7-foot-1, Philadelphia Warrior

High Flyers

The most astonishing dunkers are the high flyers, who charge toward the basket and "fly" into the air. Some make reverse moves, change hands, or go over and around other players while flying.

Julius "Dr. J." Erving was one of the early high flyers. He once took off from the free-throw line (that's 15 feet from the basket) and sailed all the way to the basket for the dunk!

Dr. J. could jump so high that he could get up above the outstretched arms of defensive players and slam the ball through the basket.

Julius Erving, 6-foot-7, Philadelphia 76ers

Michael "Air" Jordan is a great jumper and an exciting slam dunker. But what really sets him apart is his "hang time"—how long he stays in the air.

Sometimes Michael makes several moves in the air before dunking. If he jumps up to slam with his left hand and an opponent tries to block him, Michael can switch to his right hand and go around or through the opponent's waving arms. When he's clear, still "hanging," Michael finishes the dunk.

Michael Jordan, 6-foot-6, Chicago Bulls

One of the best young dunkers in the NBA today is Shawn Kemp. Shawn jumps so easily that it sometimes looks as if he's flying!

When he was a teenager, Shawn played basketball on a playground in Elkhart, Indiana. According to his cousin, Shawn once dunked the ball so hard through a basket with a chain net that sparks flew!

Shawn Kemp, 6-foot-10, Seattle SuperSonics

Dominique Wilkins usually starts his dunks close to the basket. Because he jumps so high and gets up into the air quickly, Dominique can dunk from either side of the basket.

Dominique has won two slam-dunk contests. He even beat Michael Jordan once by jumping into the air, turning a complete circle, and then slamming the ball through the basket!

Dominique Wilkins, 6-foot-8, Atlanta Hawks

Clyd...
the bas...
nickna...
One re...
so gra...
holds...
over ...
the ba...

Cly...
jump...
was ...
inche...
with...

Clyde Drexler, 6-foot-7, Portland Trail Blazers

Power Dunkers

The biggest and strongest players slam with such force that opponents scatter as the ball rockets through the net. Until the NBA created more flexible rims, which bend and snap back into place, some players dunked so hard that they ripped the basket right off the backboard!

Patrick Ewing uses a variety of power dunks. One of his favorites is the one-hand reverse dunk. With his back to the basket, Patrick slams the ball over his head. He's so big that it's almost impossible to block the shot.

Patrick Ewing, 7-foot-0, New York Knicks

As one of the few left-handers in the NBA, David Robinson is famous for his swooping left-handed slams.

During the 1991 and 1992 seasons, David had more dunks than any player in the league. He once dunked 12 times in a single game. That's 24 points on slam dunks alone!

David Robinson, 7-foot-1, San Antonio Spurs

Charles Barkley is 6-foot-6, only a medium height for a basketball player. But he is one of the NBA's top power dunkers because he is such a strong jumper. Great power dunkers need strong legs to get up into the air, plus strong shoulders and arms to slam.

Charles once dunked so hard that the basket support slid 6 inches. The basket support weighs a ton, as much as an elephant!

Charles Barkley, 6-foot-6, Phoenix Suns, formerly with the Philadelphia 76ers

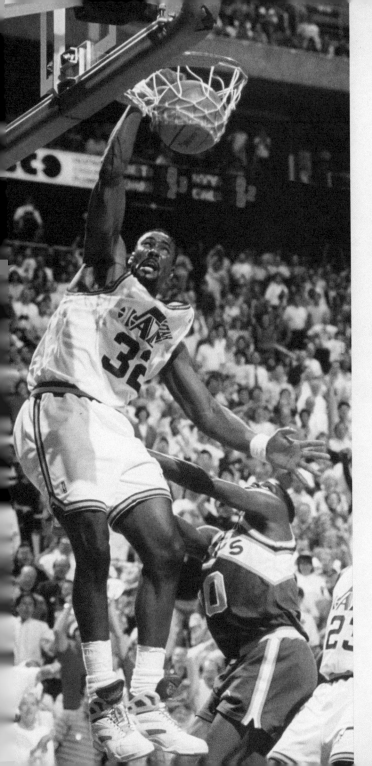

Karl Malone's most powerful dunks come when he's sprinting down the court ahead of the other team. This is called a "fast break." Karl runs so fast that when he goes up for the dunk, he continues to fly right under the basket. Sometimes the ball goes through the net and bounces off his shoulder!

Karl Malone, 6-foot-9, Utah Jazz

Dan Majerle dunks with such force that teammates call him "Thunder Dan."

Actually Dan does just about everything well. Not only is he one of the NBA's best dunkers, but he is a good shooter, passer, and defensive player as well. That's why his coach uses Dan at two positions—guard and forward.

Dan Majerle, 6-foot-6, Phoenix Suns

Buck Williams is another big power dunker who relies on size and strength.

A strong player around the basket, Buck gets many of his slams on offensive rebounds. When one of his teammates misses a shot, Buck grabs the rebound. He slams it through the net or goes back up for a two-handed dunk.

Buck Williams, 6-foot-8, Portland Trail Blazers

Little Big Men

Until 1984 all the great dunkers were tall—at least 6 feet. That's because the basket is 10 feet off the ground. But then Spud Webb, only 5-foot-7, proved that even the shortest players can slam if they are able to jump high enough.

Spud won the Gatorade Slam-Dunk Championship in Dallas in 1985. He used a variety of two-handed slams to beat players at least a foot taller.

Maybe the funniest slam dunk of all was when Spud drove to the hoop, slammed the ball through the net, and landed under the basket. The ball bounced off his head and right back out through the basket!

Spud Webb, 5-foot-7, Sacramento Kings, formerly with the Atlanta Hawks

Dee Brown is another short player who has won the Gatorade Slam-Dunk Championship. Dee is only 6-foot-1, but he can do almost as many different dunks as Michael Jordan, who is 6-foot-6.

Brown's most famous dunk came in the 1990 slam-dunk contest. High in the air, Dee covered his eyes with his right hand and then slammed with his left. He called it the "no look" dunk.

Dee Brown, 6-foot-1, Boston Celtics

Johnny Dawkins has never won a slam-dunk title, but he's still a great dunker for his size.

Just 6-foot-1 and weighing 170 pounds, Johnny relies on quickness and speed when going in for a slam. His speed helps him get past taller players and drive to the basket. Once there, Johnny gets up into the air as quickly as any player in the league.

Johnny Dawkins, 6-foot-1, Philadelphia 76ers

Byron Scott, a great shooter, is also known for his high-flying dunking. Byron's powerful legs propel him high into the air and allow him to glide past defenders.

Byron can also take off fast enough to finish a dunk, even against much bigger players. That's why Byron was one of Magic Johnson's favorite targets for passes when the two were teammates on the Los Angeles Lakers.

Byron Scott, 6-foot-4, Los Angeles Lakers

Although he is a great jumper, speed is what makes Kenny Smith such a spectacular dunker.

Kenny is one of the fastest players in the NBA when it comes to dribbling the ball up the court. That's why he's very dangerous on the fast break—dribbling past bigger players to the basket, flying into the air, and slamming the ball through the hoop.

Kenny Smith, 6-foot-3, Houston Rockets

The Future

Players such as Billy Owens, Larry Johnson, and Stacey Augmon were rookies during the 1992-1993 season, but they are already among the best dunkers in the NBA.

Billy Owens can play every position except center! Although most tall players aren't very good ballhandlers, Billy, who is 6-foot-9, handles the ball well enough to play guard. He's also strong enough to play power forward, and that's where his dunking ability is important.

Billy can slam with either hand, finish a fast break with a one-hand slam, or dunk a rebound with a two-handed slam.

Billy Owens, 6-foot-9, Golden State Warriors

Larry Johnson, 6-foot-7, Charlotte Hornets

Stacey Augmon, 6-foot-8, Atlanta Hawks

Larry Johnson and Stacey Augmon were college teammates before they entered the NBA. Larry is often compared to Charles Barkley because of his size and strength.

But Larry, who is 6-foot-7, might become an even better dunker than Charles, since he can slam with either hand.

Like David Robinson and Johnny Dawkins, Stacey is left-handed. At 6-foot-8, Stacey is one of the tallest guards in the league. His height, speed, and jumping ability also make Stacey one of the NBA's best young defensive players.

Is Basketball in Your Future?

All of the best basketball players have many of the same abilities. They spend hours practicing their passing, shooting, and dribbling skills. They also study the moves of great professional players.

That's what you need to do if you are thinking about a future in basketball. First learn the basic skills. Practice dribbling with both hands and learn to shoot from all over the floor. Also practice jumping and do exercises to keep your legs strong.

Then—if you stick with it—maybe you, too, will become a great slam dunker!